Wyoming

D0376261

Wyoming

BARRY GIFFORD

SEVEN STORIES PRESS

New York • London • Toronto • Melbourne

Copyright © 2000 by Barry Gifford
First Trade Paperback Edition, May 2004

Line drawings by Barry Gifford

Portions of this book appeared, in a different form,
in the magazine *Speak, San Francisco*, edited by Dan Rolleri.

p. 52: "Lucille" by Richard Penniman and Albert Collins. © 1960 Sony/ATV Songs
LLC. (Renewed) All Rights Reserved, Used by Permission. All rights administered
by Sony/ATV Music Publishing, 8 Music Square West, Nashville, TN 37203.

p. 125: "Java Jive" by Milton Drake and Ben Oakland. © 1940 Warner Bros. Inc., ©
renewed 1968 Warner Bros. Inc. and Sony Tunes Inc. All Rights outside the USA
controlled by Warner Bros. Inc. All Rights Reserved. Used by Permission. Warner
Bros. Publications U.S. Inc., Miami, FL 33014

All rights reserved. No part of this book may be reproduced, stored in a
retrieval system, or transmitted in any form, by any means, including
mechanical, electronic, photocopying, recording or otherwise,
without the prior written permission of the publisher.

Seven Stories Press
140 Watts Street
New York, NY 10013
http://www.sevenstories.com/

IN CANADA
Publishers Group Canada, 250A Carlton Street, Toronto, ON M5A 2L1

IN THE UK
Turnaround Publisher Services Ltd., Unit 3, Olympia Trading Estate, Coburg Road,
Wood Green, London N22 6TZ

IN AUSTRALIA
Palgrave Macmillan, 627 Chapel Street, South Yarra VIC 3141

LIBRARY OF CONGRESS CATALOGING-IN-PUBLICATION DATA
Gifford, Barry, 1946–
Wyoming : a novel / Barry Gifford.— 1st trade paperback ed.
p. cm.
ISBN 1-58322-636-2 (pbk. : alk. paper)
1. Automobile travel—Fiction. 2. Separation (Psychology)—Fiction.
3. Mothers and sons—Fiction. 4. Runaway wives—Fiction. 5. Boys—Fiction. I. Title.
PS3557.I283W96 2004
813'.54—dc22
2004007762

College professors may order examination copies of Seven Stories Press titles
for a free six-month trial period. To order, visit www.sevenstories.com/textbook/
or fax on school letterhead to 212.226.1411.

Book design by India Amos

Printed in Canada
9 8 7 6 5 4 3 2 1

Contents

Recuerdos, Chaparrita,
recuerdos y sueños

Roy's Map

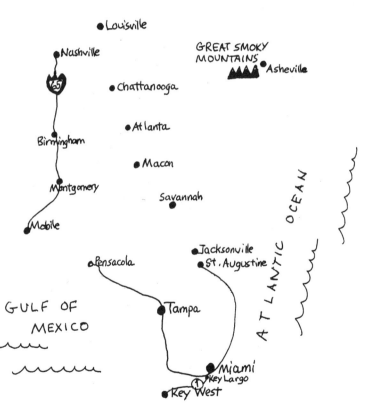

Indianapolis

● Louisville

● Nashville

GREAT SMOKY
MOUNTAINS
▲▲▲▲ ● Asheville

I-65

● Chattanooga

● Atlanta

Birmingham

● Macon

Montgomery

Savannah

● Mobile

● Jacksonville
● St. Augustine

● Pensacola

ATLANTIC OCEAN

GULF OF
MEXICO

● Tampa

● Miami
● Key Largo
① ● Key West

● Havana

Wyoming

Cobratown

"We're really fine when we're together, aren't we? I mean, when it's just the two of us."

"Uh-huh. How long till we get to the reptile farm?"

"Oh, less than an hour, I think."

"Will they have a giant king cobra, like on the sign?"

"I'm sure they will, sweetheart."

"I hope it's not asleep when we get there. Mom, do cobras sleep?"

"Of course, snakes have to sleep just like people. At least I think they do."

"Do they think?"

"Who, baby?"

"Snakes. Do they have a brain?"

"Yes. They think about food, mostly. What they're going to eat next in order to survive."

"They only think about eating?"

"That's the main thing. And finding a warm, safe place to sleep."

"Some snakes live in trees, on the branches. That can't be so safe. Birds can get them."

"They wait on the limbs for prey, some smaller creature to come along and the snake can snatch it up, or drop on it and wrap itself around and squeeze it to death or until it passes out from not having enough air to breathe. Then the snake crushes it and devours it."

"You're a good driver, aren't you, Mom? You like to drive."

"I'm a very good driver, Roy. I like to drive when we go on long trips together."

"How far is it from Key West to Mississippi?"

I

"Well, to Jackson, where we're going, it's a pretty long way. Several hundred miles. We go north through Florida, then across Alabama to Mississippi and up to Jackson, which is about in the middle of the state."

"Will Dad be there?"

"No, honey. Your dad is in Chicago. At least I think he is. He could be away somewhere on business."

"Who are we going to see in Mississippi?"

"A good friend of Mommy's. A man named Bert."

"Why is Bert in Mississippi?"

"That's where he lives, baby. He owns a hotel in Jackson."

"What's the name of the hotel?"

"The Prince Rupert."

"Is it like the Casa Azul?"

"I think Bert's hotel is bigger."

"You've never seen it?"

"No, only a photo of it on a postcard that Bert sent."

"How old is Bert?"

"I'm not sure. I guess about forty."

"How old is Dad?"

"Forty-three. He'll be forty-four next month, on the tenth of April."

"Will he invite me to his birthday party?"

"I don't know if your dad will have a birthday party, Roy, but I'm sure he would invite you if he did."

"Some dinosaurs had two brains, Mom, do you know that?"

"Two brains?"

"Yeah, there's a picture in my dinosaur book that Dad sent me that shows how the really big ones had a regular-size brain in their head and a small one in their tail. The really big ones. It's because it was so far from their head to their tail there was too much for only one brain to think about, so God gave them two."

"Who told you God gave dinosaurs two brains?"

"Nanny."

"Your grandmother doesn't know anything about dinosaurs."

"What about Bert?"

"What about him?"

"Do you think he knows about dinosaurs?"

"You'll have to ask him, baby. I don't really know what Bert knows about."

"You said he was your friend."

"Yes, he is."

"Why don't I know him?"

"He's kind of a new friend. That's why I'm taking you to Jackson, to meet Bert, so he can be your friend, too."

"Is Bert a friend of Dad's?"

"No, baby. Dad doesn't know Bert."

"How far now to the reptile farm?"

"We're pretty close. The last sign said twenty-six miles. I can't go too fast on this road."

"I like this car, Mom. I like that it's blue and white, like the sky, except now there's dark clouds."

"It's called a Holiday."

"We're on a holiday now, right?"

"Yes, Roy, it's a kind of holiday. Just taking a little trip, the two of us."

"We're pals, huh?"

"We sure are, baby. You're my best pal."

"Better than Bert?"

"Yes, darling, better than anyone else. You'll always be my favorite boy."

"Look, Mom! We must be really close now."

"The sign said, 'Ten minutes to Cobratown.'"

"If it rains hard, will the snakes stay inside?"

"It's only raining a little, Roy. They'll be out. They'll all be out, baby, don't worry. There'll be cobras crawling all over Cobratown, just for us. You'll see."

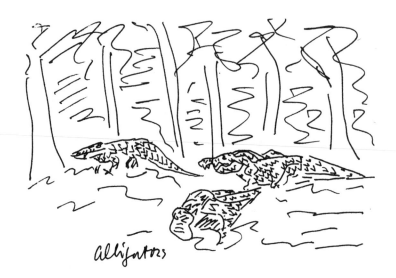

alligators

Chinese Down the Amazon

"*What do you think, baby?* Does this place look all right to you?"

"Is it safe?"

"Safe as any motel room in Alabama can be, I guess. At least it looks clean."

"And it doesn't stink of old cigarettes, like the last one."

"We can stay here."

"I'm tired, Mom."

"Take off your shoes and lie down, baby. I'll go out and bring back something for dinner. I'll bet there's a Chinese restaurant in this town. There's Chinese everywhere, Roy, you know that? Even down the Amazon it said in the *National Geographic*. I can get some egg rolls and pork chow mein and egg foo yung. What do you think, baby? Would you like some chow mein and egg foo yung? I'll just make a quick stop in the bathroom first. Out in a jiffy."

"Could I get a Coca-Cola?"

"Oh! Oh, Christ! This is disgusting! Come on, baby, we're moving."

"What happened, Mom?"

"Just filth! The bathroom is crazy with cockroaches! Even the toilet's filled with bugs!"

"I don't see any bugs on the bed."

"Those kind come out later, when the light's off. Get off of there! The beds are probably infested, too. Let's go!"

"I've got to put on my shoes."

"You can do it in the car. Come on!"

"Mom?"

"Yes, Roy?"

"Could I get a hamburger instead of Chinese?"

Bandages

"*I was very shy when I was a girl*, so shy it was painful. When I had to leave my room at school, to go to class, I often became physically ill. I got sick at the thought of having to see people, or their having to see me, to talk to them. I think this is why I had my skin problems, my eczema. It came from nerves. Being sick allowed me to stay by myself, wrapped up in bandages. People left me alone."

"But weren't you lonely?"

"Not really. I liked to read and listen to the radio and dream. I didn't have to be asleep to really dream, to go into another world where I wasn't afraid of meeting people, of having them look at me and judge me. I really felt better, safe, inside those bandages. They were my shield, I suppose, my protection."

"Prince Valiant has a shield."

"I like this song, Roy. Listen, I'll turn it up: Dean Martin singing 'Ain't Love a Kick in the Head.' He works hard to sound so casual, so relaxed. I always had the feeling Dean Martin was really very shy, like me. That he affected this style of not seeming to care, to be so cool, in order to cover up his real feelings. That's his shield."

"Are we still in Indiana?"

"Yes, baby. We'll be in Indianapolis soon. We'll stay there tonight."

"Indiana goes on a long time."

"It seems that way sometimes. Look out the window. Maybe you'll see a farmer."

"Mom, are there still Indians in Indiana?"

"I don't think so, baby. They all moved away."

"Then why is it still called Indiana, if there aren't any Indians left?"

7

"Just because they were here before. There were Indians, many different tribes, all over the country."

"The Indians rode horses. They didn't have cars."

"Some of them had cars after."

"After what?"

"After people came from Europe."

"They brought cars from Europe?"

"Yes, but they made them here, too. That's where the Indians got them, the same as everybody else."

"There aren't so many horses here as in Florida."

"Probably not."

"Mom?"

"Yes, Roy?"

"You still wrap yourself up with bandages sometimes."

"When I have an attack of eczema, to cover the ointment I put on the sores, so I don't get everything greasy."

"You don't want anyone to see the sores?"

"One time, not long after I married your father, I had such a bad attack that my skin turned red and black, and I had to stay in the hospital for a month. The sores got so bad they bled. The skin on my arms and hands and face stank under the bandages. I couldn't wash and I smelled terrible. When the nurses unwrapped the bandages to sponge me off, the odor made me want to vomit.

"One day your dad's brother, Uncle Bruno, was there when the nurses took off the bandages. He didn't believe I was really sick, I don't know why, but he wanted to see for himself. It was costing your dad a lot of money for doctors to take care of me and to keep me in a private hospital. When they removed my bandages, Bruno was horrified by the sight of my skin. He couldn't stand the smell or to look at me, and he ran out of the room. I guess he was worried about all the money your father was spending on me. He probably thought I was pretending to be so sick. After that, he said to your dad, 'Kitty used to be so beautiful. What happened to her?'"

"But you are beautiful, Mom."

"I wasn't then, baby, not when I was so sick. I looked pretty bad. But

Bruno knew I wasn't faking. I screamed when the nurse peeled off the bandages, my skin stuck to them. Bruno heard me. He wanted your dad to get rid of me, I was too much trouble."

"Did Dad want to get rid of you?"

"No, baby, he didn't. We separated for other reasons."

"Was I a reason?"

"No, sweetheart, of course you weren't. Your father loves you more than anything, just like I do. You mustn't ever think that. The trouble was just between your dad and me, it had nothing to do with you. Really, you're the most precious thing to both of us."

"When will we get to Chicago?"

"Tomorrow afternoon."

"Where are we going to stay? At Nanny's house?"

"No, baby, we'll stay at the hotel, the same place as before. Remember how you like the chocolate sundaes they make in the restaurant there?"

"Uh-huh. Can we sit in the big booth by the window when we have breakfast?"

"Sure, baby."

"Can I have a chocolate sundae for breakfast?"

"One time you can, okay?"

"Okay."

"Mom?"

"Huh?"

"Do I have nerves?"

"What do you mean, baby? Everyone has nerves."

"I mean, will I ever have to be wrapped up in bandages because of my nerves?"

"No, Roy, you won't. You're not nervous like I was, like I sometimes get now only not so bad as when I was younger. It'll never happen to you, never. Don't worry."

"I love you, Mom. I hope you never have sores and have to get wrapped up again."

"I hope so, too, baby. And remember, I love you more than anything."

Soul Talk

"Mom, when birds die, what happens to their souls?"

"What made you think of that, Roy?"

"I was watching a couple of crows fly by."

"You think birds have souls?"

"That's what Nanny says."

"What do you think the soul is, baby?"

"Something inside a person."

"Where inside?"

"Around the middle."

"You mean by the heart?"

"I don't know. Someplace deep. Can a doctor see it on an X ray?"

"No, baby, nobody can see it. Sometimes you can feel your soul yourself. It's just a feeling. Not everybody has one."

"Some people don't have a soul?"

"I don't know, Roy, but there are more than a few I'll bet have never been in touch with theirs. Or who'd recognize it if it glowed in the dark."

"Can you see your soul in the dark if you take off all your clothes and look in the mirror?"

"Only if your eyes are closed."

"Mom, that doesn't make sense."

"I hate to tell you this, baby, but the older you get and the more you figure things should make sense, they more than sometimes don't."

"Your soul flies away like a crow when you die and hides in a cloud. When it rains that means the clouds are full of souls and some of 'em are squeezed out. Rain is the dead souls there's no more room for in heaven."

"Did Nanny tell you this, Roy?"

"No, it's just something I thought."

"Baby, there's no way I'll ever think about rain the same way again."

Skylark

"You know, sometimes you look just like your father, only much more beautiful, of course."

"You don't think Dad is beautiful?"

"No, your father isn't so beautiful, but he's a real man."

"And I'm a real boy, like Pinocchio wanted to be."

"Yes, baby, you're a real boy."

"Why isn't Dad with us so much anymore?"

"He's very busy, Roy, you know that. His business takes up most of his time."

"When will I see him again?"

"We'll go to Havana in two weeks and meet him there. You like the hotel where his apartment is, remember? The Nacional?"

"Will the little man with the curly white dog be there?"

"Little man? Oh, Mr. Lipsky. I don't know, baby. Remember the last time we saw him? In Miami, the day after the big hurricane."

"We were walking down the middle of the street that looked like it was covered with diamonds, and Mr. Lipsky was carrying his dog."

"The hurricane had blown out most of the windows of the big hotels, and Collins Avenue was paved with chunks of glass."

"Mr. Lipsky kissed you. I remember he had to stand on his toes. Then he gave me a piece of candy."

"He was carrying his tiny dog because he didn't want him to cut his paws on the broken glass. Mr. Lipsky said the dog was used to taking a walk every morning at that time and he didn't want to disappoint him."

"Mr. Lipsky talks funny."

"What do you mean, he talks funny?"

"He sings."

"Sings?"

"Like he's singing a little song when he says something to you."

"Sure, baby, I know what you mean. Mr. Lipsky's a little odd, but he's been a good friend to your dad and us."

"Does Mr. Lipsky have a wife?"

"I think so, but I've never met her."

"I hope when I grow up I won't be as little as him."

"*As he*, honey. *As* little as *he*. Of course you won't. You'll be as tall as your dad, or taller."

"Is Mr. Lipsky rich?"

"Why do you ask that, baby?"

"Because he always wears those big sparkly rings."

"Well, Roy, Mr. Lipsky is probably one of the wealthiest men in America."

"How did he get so rich?"

"Oh, he has lots of different kinds of businesses, here and in Cuba. All over the world, maybe."

"What kinds of businesses?"

"Lots of times he gives people money to start a business, and then they have to pay him back more than the amount he gave them or pay him part of what they earn for as long as the business lasts."

"I guess he's pretty smart."

"Your dad thinks Mr. Lipsky is the smartest man he's ever met."

"I hope I'm smart."

"You are, Roy. Don't worry about being smart."

"You know what, Mom?"

"What, baby?"

"I think if I had to choose one thing, to be tall or to be smart, I'd take smart."

"You'll be both, sweetheart, you won't have to choose."

"Do you know what Mr. Lipsky's dog's name is?"

"Sky something, isn't it? Skylark, that's it, like the Hoagy Carmichael song."

"I bet he's smart, too. A dog named Skylark would have to be very smart."

Flamingos

"*Mom, after I die* I want to come back as a flamingo."

"You won't die for a very long time, Roy. It's too soon to be thinking about it. But I'm not so sure that after people die they come back at all. How do you know about reincarnation? And why a flamingo?"

"How do I know about what?"

"Reincarnation. Like you said, some people believe that after they die they'll return in a different form, as another person or even as an insect or animal."

"Mammy Yerma told me it could happen."

"Mammy Yerma usually knows what she's talking about, but I'm not so sure about being reincarnated, even as a flamingo."

"Flamingos are the most beautiful birds, like the ones around the pond at the racetrack in Hialeah. I'd like to be a dark pink flamingo with a really long, curvy neck."

"They're elegant birds, baby, that's for sure."

"If you could come back as an animal, Mom, what would you be?"

"A leopard, probably. Certainly a big cat of some kind, if I had a choice. Leopards are strong and fast and beautiful. They climb trees, Roy, did you know that? Leopards are terrifically agile."

"What's agile?"

"They're great leapers, with perfect balance. They can jump up in a tree and walk along a narrow limb better than the best acrobat. Another thing about leopards, I believe, is that they mate for life."

"What's that mean?"

"It means once a male and female leopard start a family, they stay together until they die,"

"People do, too."

"Yes, baby, some people do. But I think it's harder for human beings to remain true to one another than it is for leopards."

"Why?"

"Well, all animals have to worry about is getting food, protecting their young, and to avoid being eaten by bigger animals. Humans have much more to deal with, plus our brain is different. A leopard acts more on instinct, what he feels. A person uses his brain to reason, to decide what to do."

"I'd like to be a leopard with a human brain. Then I could leap up in a tree and read a book and nobody would bother me because they'd be afraid."

"Baby, are you getting hungry? We humans have to decide if we want to stop soon and eat."

"A leopard would probably eat a flamingo, if he was hungry enough."

"Maybe, but a skinny bird doesn't make much of a meal, and I don't think a leopard would want to mess with all of those feathers."

"Mom, I need to go to the bathroom."

"Now that's something neither a leopard nor a flamingo would think twice about. I'll stop at the next exit. I need to go, too."

Wyoming

"What's your favorite place, Mom?"

"Oh, I have a lot of favorite places, Roy. Cuba, Jamaica, Mexico."

"Is there a place that's really perfect? Somewhere you'd go if you had to spend the rest of your life there and didn't want anyone to find you?"

"How do you know that, baby?"

"Know what?"

"That sometimes I think about going someplace where nobody can find me."

"Even me?"

"No, honey, not you. We'd be together, wherever it might be."

"How about Wyoming?"

"Wyoming?"

"Have you ever been there?"

"Your dad and I were in Sun Valley once, but that's in Idaho. No, Roy, I don't think so. Why?"

"It's really big there, with lots of room to run. I looked on a map. Wyoming's probably a good place to have a dog."

"I'm sure it is, baby. You'd like to have a dog, huh?"

"It wouldn't have to be a big dog, Mom. Even a medium-size or small dog would be okay."

"When I was a little girl we had a chow named Toy, a big black Chinese dog with a long purple tongue. Toy loved everyone in the family, especially me, and he would have defended us to the death. He was dangerous to anyone outside the house, and not only to people."

"One day Nanny found two dead cats hanging over the back fence in our yard. She didn't know where they came from, and she buried them. The next day or the day after that, she found two or three more dead cats hanging over the fence. It turned out that Toy was killing the neighborhood cats and draping them over the fence to show us. After that, he had to wear a muzzle."

"What's a muzzle?"

"A mask over his mouth, so he couldn't bite. He was a great dog, though, to me. Toy loved the snow when we lived in Illinois. He loved to roll in it and sleep outside on the front porch in the winter. His long fur coat kept him warm."

"What happened to Toy?"

"He ran after a milk truck one day and was hit by a car and killed. This happened just after I went away to school. The deliveryman said that Toy was trying to bite him through the muzzle."

"Does it snow in Wyoming?"

"Oh, yes, baby, it snows a lot in Wyoming. It gets very cold there."

"Toy would have liked it."

"I'm sure he would."

"Mom, can we drive to Wyoming?"

"You mean now?"

"Uh-huh. Is it far?"

"Very far. We're almost to Georgia."

"Can we go someday?"

"Sure, Roy, we'll go."

"We won't tell anyone, right, Mom?"

"No, baby, nobody will know where we are."

"And we'll have a dog."

"I don't see why not."

"From now on when anything bad happens, I'm going to think about Wyoming. Running with my dog."

"It's a good thing, baby. Everybody needs Wyoming."

Saving the Planet

"Mom, what would happen if there was no sun?"

"People couldn't live, plants wouldn't grow. The planet would freeze and become a gigantic ball of ice."

"In school they said the earth is shaped like a pear, not round like a ball."

"So it would be a huge frozen pear spinning out of control. The planets in our solar system revolve around the sun, Roy. If the sun burned out, Earth and Mars and Venus and Saturn and all the others would just be hurtling through space until they crashed into meteors or one another."

"Will it ever happen?"

"What, baby?"

"That there won't be any sun?"

"I don't think so. Not in our lifetime, anyway. Oh, Roy, look at the horses! Nothing is more beautiful than horses running in open country like that."

"Dad's never going to live with us again, is he?"

"I'm not sure, baby. We'll have to wait and see. You'll see your father, though, no matter what."

"I know, Mom. I just hope you're right about the sun not burning out."

21

A Nice Day on the Ocean

"You know that friend of Dad's with one eye that's always mostly closed?"

"Buzzy Shy. His real name is Enzo Buozzi. What about him?"

"A waiter at the Saxony said Buzzy wanted to give him five dollars to let him kiss his fly."

"Who told you that?"

"I heard him tell Eddie C."

"Heard who?"

"Freddy, the waiter. Why would Buzzy want to kiss Freddy's fly?"

"Did Buzzy ever touch you, Roy?"

"He pinched me once on the cheek when I brought him a cigar Dad gave me to hand him. He gave me a quarter, then tried to pinch my face again, but I got away. It hurt."

"Buzzy Shy is sick, baby. Stay away from him. Promise?"

"Promise. He doesn't look sick."

"The sickness is in his brain, so you can't see it."

"Eddie C. said for *ten* dollars Buzzy could kiss his ass and anything else."

"Who's Eddie C.?"

"A lifeguard. I think at the Spearfish."

"These aren't nice boys, Roy. I don't want you talking to them."

"I wasn't talking to them, Mom, I was listening."

"Don't listen to them, either. I'll talk to your dad about it. I don't want Buzzy Shy bothering you."

"Dad and Buzzy are friends."

"Not really. Buzzy helps out sometimes, that's all."

23

"How did his eye get like that?"

"He was a prizefighter. Somebody shut it for him."

"Maybe his brain got hurt, too."

"I don't know, baby. He was probably born with the problem in his head. Don't go near him again."

"Mom?"

"Yes, baby?"

"I like the sky like this, when it's really red with only a tiny yellow line under it."

"Red sky at night, sailor's delight. Red sky at morning, sailor take warning."

"What's that mean?"

"Tomorrow will be a nice day on the ocean."

"Sailor's Delight would be a good name for a red Popsicle, don't you think, Mom?"

"Yes, Roy, I do. Remember to tell your dad. I'm sure he knows someone in the Popsicle business."

Perfect Spanish

"Before you were born, I got very sick and your dad made me go to Cuba to recover. I stayed in a lovely house on a beach next to a lavish estate. It was a perfect cure for me, lying in the sun, without responsibilities."

"Was Dad with you?"

"No, I was alone. There was a Chinese couple who took care of the house and me. Chang and Li were their names."

"How long were you there?"

"Six weeks. I was so happy, just by myself, reading, resting, swimming in the Caribbean Sea. It really was the best time of my life. I never felt better, until, of course, I had to leave."

"Why did you have to leave?"

"To make sure you were a healthy baby. I needed to be near my doctor, who was in Chicago."

"The ground is so beautiful here, Mom. It looks like snow, but the air is very hot."

"That's cotton, baby. Cotton is the main crop in Alabama. The temperature doesn't stay high long enough up north to grow it there. Also, the cost of labor is much cheaper in the South, and picking cotton is extremely labor-intensive."

"What does that mean?"

"It takes a lot of people to handpick the buds. That's why slaves were brought here from Africa, to work in the fields."

"They didn't want to come."

"No, baby, they didn't."

"There aren't slaves now, though, right?"

"Not officially, no. But too many people still live almost the same way as they did a hundred or more years ago. There's no work here, really, except in the cottonfields, and it doesn't pay much. The difference between then and now is that people are free to come and go, they're not owned by another person."

"I wouldn't like to be owned by someone."

"Nobody does. Slavery is against the law in the United States, but it still exists in some parts of the world."

"Let's not go there."

"We won't, Roy, I promise."

"Were there slaves in Cuba?"

"At one time, yes."

"Were there slaves when you were there before I was born?"

"No, baby, that was only a few years ago."

"Chang and Li weren't slaves, right?"

"Certainly not. They were caretakers of the property. Chang and Li were very happy to be working there. They were wonderful people and very kind to me."

"How did they get from China to Cuba?"

"I don't know. By boat, probably. Or maybe their parents came from China and Chang and Li were born in Cuba. They spoke perfect Spanish.

"Roy?"

"Yeah, Mom?"

"Are you all right?"

"I'm okay."

"Something's bothering you, I can tell. What is it?"

"I think I'd like to learn to speak perfect Spanish."

"You can, baby. You can start taking Spanish lessons whenever you want."

"Mom?"

"Yes, sweetheart?"

"I bet the slaves didn't think the cotton fields were so beautiful."

Seconds

*"**Are we going to see** Pops and Nanny soon?"*

"Yes, baby, we'll be in New Orleans for three or four days, then we'll go to Miami. I don't know if Pops will be there, but Nanny will."

"Why isn't Pops there so much?"

"I never told you this before, but I think you're old enough now to understand. Pops and Nanny haven't always been together. There was a time when I was a girl—more than ten years, in fact—when they were each married to another person."

"Who were they married to?"

"Nanny's husband was a man named Tim O'Malley. His family was in the trucking business in Chicago. Pops married a woman named Sally Price, and they lived in Kansas City. I used to go down on the train and visit them there. This was from when I was the age you are now until I went away to college."

"Why did they marry other people?"

"In those days Pops was a traveling salesman for a shoe company, and Kansas City was part of his territory. Sally was a girlfriend of his for a couple of years before Pops and Nanny got divorced. When he decided to spend more time with Sally than with Nanny, my mother divorced him and she married O'Malley, who'd always liked her."

"So O'Malley was like your other father."

"In a way, but we were never close. I lived most of the time at boarding school, Our Lady of Angelic Desire, so I didn't really see him so much. He died suddenly of a heart attack ten years to the day after he and your grandmother were married."

"How did she and Pops get back together?"

27

"Pops had divorced Sally two years before O'Malley's death and moved back to Illinois. He always loved my mother and would stand across the street sometimes to watch her come out of our house and get in her car and drive away. Pops wanted Nanny back, and after O'Malley was gone, she agreed to remarry him."

"I bet you were happy."

"No, I wasn't particularly happy, because I didn't completely understand why Pops had left in the first place. O'Malley was nothing special to me, and he wasn't as smart or funny or handsome as my father, but my mother blamed Pops for their separation and I guess I took her side, right or wrong. I don't feel the same way now. It's difficult to know what really goes on between people in a marriage, and I don't think anyone other than those two people can understand, including their children."

"What about you and Dad?"

"What about us, Roy?"

"You're divorced but you're still friends, aren't you?"

"Oh, yes, baby, your dad and I are very good friends. We're better friends now than when we were married."

"And you both love me."

"Of course, baby. Both your dad and I would do anything for you."

"It's okay with me that you and Dad don't live together, but sometimes I get afraid that I won't see him anymore."

"You can see your dad whenever you like. When we get to the hotel in New Orleans, we'll call him, okay? I think he's in Las Vegas now. Maybe he can come to see us before he goes back to Chicago."

"Yeah, Mom, let's call him. Remember the last time we were with him in New Orleans and he ate too many oysters and got so sick?"

"We'll make sure he doesn't eat oysters this time, don't worry. Try to sleep a little now, baby. I'll wake you up when we get there."

Roy's World

"Remember the time you caught a barracuda and brought it back to the hotel and asked Pete the chef to cook it for you?"

"It was the first fish I ever caught. I was out with Uncle Jack on Captain Jimmy's boat, fishing for grouper, but a 'cuda took my mullet."

"Pete thought you were so cute, bringing the barracuda wrapped in newspaper into the kitchen. You were only five then."

"He told me that barracudas aren't good eating, so he made me a kingfish instead."

"Grilled in butter and garlic."

"And he said he wouldn't charge us for it since I'd brought him a fish to trade."

"You really love your Uncle Jack, don't you, baby?"

"He's a great fisherman, and he knows everything about boats."

"You know he was a commander in the navy?"

"Sure, he told me about how he built bridges and navy bases in the Pacific during the war."

"Uncle Jack is a civil and mechanical engineer, Roy. He can draw plans, too, like an architect. He was a Seabee, and the navy offered to make him an admiral if he stayed in."

"Why didn't he?"

"He said to make money it was better to be in private industry. That's why he moved to Florida, to build houses. My brother can do anything, though."

"He can't fly."

"What do you mean, baby? You mean like Superman?"

"No, Uncle Jack told me he tried to become a pilot in the navy. They sent him to Texas to learn how to fly, but he washed out. He said there was something wrong with his ears that made him lose his balance."

"Yes, that's right. I remember when he came home from Texas. He was so disappointed. But Jack can do so many things. You know, baby, if you get really interested in something, you should follow it through all the way. I mean, find out everything you can, learn all there is to learn about it, try to do it or figure it out. That's what your Uncle Jack does, that's how come he knows so much about different things. He can't do everything so well, like flying a plane, but he tries. And you know he's been practically all over the world. Jack's a great traveler."

"I'm going to be a great traveler, too. We travel a lot, don't we, Mom?"

"Yes, we do, but except for Cuba and Mexico, only in the United States."

"I like to draw maps."

"You mean to copy them from the atlas?"

"Sometimes, just to learn where places are. But also I like to make countries up. Oceans and seas, too. It's fun to invent a world nobody else knows."

"What's your favorite country that you made up?"

"Turbania. It's full of tribes of warriors who're always fighting to take over all of Turbania. The largest tribe is the Forestani. They live in the mountains and come down to attack the Vashtis and Saladites, who are desert people."

"Where exactly is Turbania?"

"Between Nafili and Durocq, on the Sea of Kazmir. A really fierce small tribe, the Bazini, live in the port city of Purset. They're very rich because they own the port and have a big wall all around with fortifications not even the Forestanis can penetrate. The Bazinis also have rifles, which the other tribes don't. The Vashtis and Saladites ride horses, black and white Arabians. The Forestanis travel on foot because the woods in the hills are so thick that horses can't get through. And each tribe has its own language, though the Bazinis speak Spanish and maybe English, too, because of the shipping trade. The Forestanis can also speak like birds, which is the way they communicate when they don't want anyone outside the tribe to know what they're saying. It's a secret language that they're forbidden by tribal law to teach outsiders. If a Forestani is caught telling the secret bird language to a person from another tribe, his tongue is cut out and his eardrums are punctured."

"Well, Roy, we'll be in Chattanooga soon. Let's have a snack and you can tell me about some of your other countries. I hope they're not all as terrible as Turbania."

"Turbania's not so terrible, Mom. Wait until you hear about Cortesia, where all the people are blind and they have to walk around with long sticks to protect themselves from bumping into things and each other, so everyone pokes everyone else with their sticks all the time."

Nomads

"Where are we now, Mom?"

"Just outside Centralia, Illinois."

"This is sure a long train."

"I'll turn off the motor. Tell me if you get too cold, Roy, and I'll turn the heater back on."

"It's cold out, but not real cold yet, even though it's almost December. Why is that?"

"Weather is pretty unpredictable sometimes, baby, especially in the spring or fall. But you can bet before too long this part of the country'll be blanketed white."

"How come we never take a train?"

"You took a train a couple of times, don't you remember? When you went up and back to Eagle River, Wisconsin."

"It was fun sleeping overnight on the train, though I didn't really sleep very much. I stayed up looking out the window into the shadows, imagining what might be out there. I like the dark, Mom, especially if I'm protected from it, like through a train window."

"What did you think you could see, Roy?"

"Monsters, of course. Lots of large creatures crunching through the forest. Then I could see campfires, real quick little flashes of smoky light burning up through the trees. I thought maybe it was Indians, the last ones left living in the woods, moving every day and setting up a new camp at night."

"Nomads."

"What's that?"

"Nomads are people who travel all the time—they don't live in one place."

"Is Nomads the name of a tribe?"

"It used to be. They're in the Bible, I think. Now it's just a word used to describe anyone who's constantly changing their place of residence."

"We move around a lot."

"Yes, we do, but we mostly stay in the same places."

"That's what the Plains Indians did. I read that they would come back to the same campgrounds depending on the seasons."

"I think the Indians understood the weather better than most people do now."

"What do you mean, Mom?"

"People live mostly in cities, so they defy the weather. They stay in their buildings and complain when it rains or snows, or that it's too hot or cold. The Indians adjusted better to changes of climate. When it was too warm on the plains, they moved to the mountains, where it was cooler. When it snowed in the mountains, they moved down."

"This train is about the longest I've ever seen."

"Cotton Belt Route. Southern Serves the South. Don't you love to read what's written on the boxcars?"

"Yeah, but what do the letters mean? Like B&O?"

"Baltimore and Ohio. L&N is Louisville and Norfolk, I think. Or maybe it's Louisiana and Norfolk."

"It's almost ending, Mom. I can see the caboose. Start the car."

"It's nice to have heat, huh, Roy? If we were Indians in the old days we would've had to wait on our horses until the train passed."

"We'd be wrapped in blankets, so we wouldn't be too cold."

"I once saw a painting of an Indian riding in a blizzard, his long-braided black hair and blanket covered with ice. Even the pony's mane was frozen."

"I like cars, Mom, but horses are more beautiful. I'd feel more like a real Nomad if I were on a horse instead of in a car. Wouldn't you?"

"I guess so, baby. But it would take us a lot longer to get anywhere."

"Sometimes I don't care how long it takes. And when we get there I'm always a little disappointed."

"Why disappointed?"

"I don't know. Maybe because sometimes it's better to imagine how something or someplace is rather than to have it or be there. That way you won't ever be disappointed when you find out it's not so great as you hoped."

"You're growing up, Roy, you really are. Some people never figure that out."

"Probably the real Nomads knew, and that's why they were always moving."

"It's impossible to avoid being disappointed sometimes, baby, unless you learn to not expect too much."

"I like traveling, Mom. I like it more than being in one place, so maybe I'm learning."

Ducks on the Pond

"Roy! Roll up your window. It's freezing outside."

"I want to leave it open just a little, okay, Mom? I like the feeling when the heater's on high and we can still feel the cold air."

"Amazing how cold it can get in Mississippi, huh, Roy? And it's not even Christmas yet."

"Where are we now?"

"We just passed the Batesville turnoff. We'll stay tonight in Memphis, maybe at the Peabody if we can get a room. Remember that hotel, baby? The one with the ducks on the pond in the lobby."

"There was a kid there the last time who told me he drowned a duck once. Not one of the Peabody ducks."

"Drowned a duck? I didn't know ducks could drown."

"I guess they can. They have to come up for air, like people, only probably not as often."

"I wish I could pass this darn truck. Sorry, Roy, I don't mean to swear, but the driver won't let me get around him. Tell me more about the ducks. Who was it who drowned one?"

"A boy I met at the Peabody Hotel the last time we stayed there. He was older than me, twelve or thirteen, I think."

"It was in March. Bert came up."

"Is Bert still alive?"

"Of course, baby. Why would you ask that?"

"Just wondering. You said he was having trouble with his brain, so I thought maybe it exploded or something."

"He had something growing in his head, that's right. You remembered. I think the doctors took it out."

"Before his brain could explode."

"His brain wouldn't have exploded, baby. At least I don't think so. If the thing that was growing in there got big enough, though, it might have squeezed the inside of Bert's head so much that he wouldn't have been able to think properly. I'll call him when we get to Memphis."

"What if the doctors couldn't get it out?"

"I'm sure they did, Roy, otherwise I would have heard something. I think I can pass now, hold on."

"Mom, where did the seed in Bert's brain come from?"

"Just a sec, baby, let me get back over into the other lane. Okay, what did you say? How did a seed get where?"

"In Bert's brain. The thing that was growing began as a seed, right? How did it get planted there?"

"That's a good question, Roy. I don't think anybody knows exactly, not even the doctors."

"Remember the Johnny Appleseed song? 'Oh, the Lord is good to me, and so I thank the Lord, for giving me the things I need, the sun and the rain and the apple seed. The Lord is good to me.'"

"I like to hear you sing, baby. You have a sweet voice."

"It couldn't have been an apple seed in Bert's head."

"No, it wasn't. Don't think about it anymore, honey. Pretty soon you'll see the ducks on the pond at the Peabody."

"Maybe that kid will be there again."

"I guess it's possible."

"I wouldn't ever try to drown a duck, even if I could."

"No, Roy, I don't believe you ever would."

Sound of the River

"Is it okay if I turn up the radio?"

"Sure, Roy, but not too loud. What's playing?"

"I don't know, but I like it."

"Is that a man or a woman who's screaming?"

"He's not screaming, Mom, he's singing. Sometimes he shouts, but it's part of the song. But that's not the part I care about so much. What I really like is the kind of thumping sound behind him, the way it jumps up around his voice sometimes and almost swallows or drowns it or something."

"You mean the rhythm section. It's the part of the band that keeps the beat. They keep the song moving."

"I don't think I've ever heard music like this before. It reminds me of the noise water makes hitting against the rocks on the side of the river, like down behind the Jax brewery. The same sound over and over, only it's not exactly the same."

"That's the Mississippi, baby. Can you remember how the waves sound on the beach in Cuba? The way they slap down on the sand, then make kind of a hushing noise as the water rushes up before rolling back. It's different than the sound of the river in New Orleans."

"I remember being out on a little boat with Uncle Jack and on one side of the boat the water was green and on the other side it was blue. Uncle Jack told me to put my right hand into the water on the starboard side, into the blue, which was really cold. Then he told me to put my left hand into the water on the port side, and it was very warm. He said the cold blue side was the ocean, and the warm green side was the Gulf Stream. Wasn't that near Varadero?"

"No, honey, that was off Key West."

"Where are we now, Mom?"

"Macon, Georgia."

"What's here?"

"Oh, most likely the same as everyplace else. Men and women who don't understand each other and aren't really willing or able to try. Just what this man is shouting about on the radio."

"I think he's saying, 'Lucille, won't you do your sister's will? Oh, Lucille, won't you do your sister's will? Well, you ran away and left, I love you still."

"Sounds about right to me."

St. Louis Cemetery, N.O.

Red Highway

"You hit one that time, Mom. I felt the bump."

"I can't avoid them all, baby. They crawl out on the road and lie there because the asphalt absorbs heat and they like the warmth. I have to admit I'm not very fond of snakes, but I'm not trying to run them over."

"I know you wouldn't do it on purpose. There are a lot of good ones, like king snakes, who help farmers by eating rodents that destroy crops."

"You've always loved reptiles, Roy. Maybe when you grow up you'll be a herpetologist."

"Is that the big word for reptile handler?"

"Herpetology is the study of snakes, and a herpetologist is a person who studies them."

"There's another one! It must be six feet long. You just missed him."

"They're easier to see when they're crawling, otherwise they blend into the highway here."

"Why is this road dark red? I've never seen a red highway before."

"It must be the earth here, baby, the color of the dirt or clay."

"If it rained now, I wonder if the snakes would all crawl away."

"Probably they'd want to get down into their holes,"

"Why were you so mean to that man in the restaurant back in Montgomery?"

"He said something I didn't care for."

"Did he say it to you?"

"No, Roy, he said it to everyone who could hear him. He *wanted* people to hear him."

41

"What was it that he said?"

"He was showing off his ignorance."

"Nobody likes a show-off."

"Especially not his kind,"

"What was he showing off about?"

"He used some words I don't like."

"He called you beautiful. 'What's the matter, beautiful?' he said."

"That wasn't what upset me. It was what he said before. Forget about him, honey. God punishes those people."

"Could God change him into a snake and make him crawl out on the red highway so he'd get run over?"

"Roy, don't believe you're better than anybody else because of the way you look or who your parents are, or for any other reason you had nothing to do with directly. Okay?"

"Okay."

"It sounds simple, but it's not so easy to do. Treat people the way you'd like them to treat you, and if you don't have anything good to say, don't say anything."

"Uh-huh."

"Sorry, baby, I don't mean to preach, but that man made me angry."

"Watch out, Mom, there's another snake!"

Lucky

"It's always raining in Indiana."

"Seems that way, doesn't it, baby?"

"I remember one night we were driving through Indiana like this and I saw a sign that said New Monster. Lucky was with us, and I asked him what it meant, and he told me there was a new monster loose around there and the sign was put up to warn people. I imagined a crazyman had escaped from an asylum, or a dangerous freak had run away from the sideshow of a carnival. I was really frightened and stayed awake for a long time staring out the window watching for the monster, even though it was dark."

"Poor Lucky. He was the one who wound up in an asylum."

"You told me he had to go to a hospital."

"He did, Roy, a special kind of hospital for people who can't control themselves."

"Lucky couldn't control himself?"

"In some ways, baby. He told terrible lies to people in business and got into trouble all the time. You know how handsome Lucky was, and he could play the piano so well and sing. When he was a young man he'd been a great athlete, too. He was a wonderful golfer and tennis player and swimmer. Lucky charmed everyone, men and women loved him, but he was insane."

"Later, Lucky told me the name on the sign was really New *Munster*, which is a town in Indiana. He was just joking around with me, Mom. That wasn't such a bad thing, even though I got so scared."

"No, of course not, baby. Lucky stole a lot of money from a big company he was working for, but he didn't go to jail for that, they let him

43

off easy. Then a few weeks later he was arrested for taking off all of his clothes in front of some young girls in a park. I guess he'd done things like that before, or he tried to do something with one of the girls, I can't remember, so this time he was committed to an institution."

"Do you know where Lucky is now?"

"I think he's still locked up in Dunning."

"Where's Dunning?"

"A place outside Chicago."

"How long does he have to stay there?"

"Oh, Roy, who knows? I suppose until he's well. It's really terrible about Lucky, it wasn't his fault. He just couldn't control himself."

"Lucky liked to eat spaghetti with a spoon. He'd chop up his noodles with a knife and then eat them with a tablespoon. Do you remember that, Mom? I think that's a crazy way to eat spaghetti."

K.C. So Far

(SECONDS/ALTERNATE TAKE)

*"**How come we've never** been to Kansas City before?"*

"I used to come here often when I was a girl. From when I was your age until I was seventeen. I rode the train back and forth from Chicago to see my father."

"Pops was in Kansas City then?"

"Yes, for a few years, when he was married to another woman. Remember, I told you about her. Actually, I don't think they were really married. They lived together and she told people they were married. I never liked her."

"What was her name?"

"I called her Aunt Sally. She was a terrible housekeeper, very sloppy. She left her clothes lying around everywhere, always had dirty dishes piled in the sink. My father liked her because she was pretty and well-read. Sally liked to talk about politics, literature, art. She wasn't stupid, I'll say that for her. She was a chain-smoker. The ashtrays in that house were always overflowing with butts and dead matches."

"It's hot here."

"It can get very hot in Kansas City, Roy, especially in the summer. We used to sit out on the porch at three and four o'clock in the morning, drinking lemonade with shaved ice, when we couldn't sleep because of the heat."

"What did Pops do in Kansas City?"

"He was a hat salesman. He traveled all over the Midwest. Traveling salesmen were still called 'drummers' back then. It's where the phrase 'drumming up business' comes from. Or maybe the word 'drummer' came from the saying, I'm not sure. I think Pops had a girlfriend in

45

every town in his territory, or most of them. That's what caused the breakup with Aunt Sally."

"Pops still wears a hat when he's outside."

"Yes, baby, a homburg, that's his favorite. Pops always was a sharp dresser."

"What happened to her?"

"Who? Sally?"

"Yeah."

"You know, I have no idea where she is now, and I doubt that Pops does, either. She stayed in Kansas City for a while after my father moved back to Chicago, then he stopped talking about her. Sally was a blonde with plenty of pep. I bet she found herself a guy and cut Pops off cold. It's strange how sometimes people can be such a large part of your life and then suddenly they're gone. I didn't miss her or those long, hot train trips."

"She wasn't nice to you, huh?"

"Sally wasn't bad to me. I guess I didn't want to like her because I was so close to Nanny, and I felt if I allowed myself to really like Sally then I would be disloyal to my mother. I'm sure most kids have the same conflict."

"If Dad got a new wife, would you want me to hate her?"

"Not at all, baby, of course not. You'd make up your own mind about her. It would depend on how she treated you."

"Even if she was nice and I loved her, I wouldn't love her the same as I love you, Mom. I'm sure I wouldn't."

"Roy, look at that airplane landing! It's coming in so low. The Kansas City airport is in the middle of the city. Planes fly in right over the houses."

"I'd be scared one would crash on us if we lived in a house here. You know, Mom, I don't think I like Kansas City so far."

Concertina Locomotion

"Sometimes it seems like things go very fast, and sometimes they go slower than an inchworm."

"Yes, honey, strange the way time moves, isn't it? I can't believe I'm not twenty or twenty-one or -two anymore. Years get lost, they fly by and you can't remember them. This is when you get older, of course. I'm sure that now you can remember almost exactly when everything happened."

"I like watching snakes crawl, the way their bodies fold and bend and curl up like a lasso, then straighten out."

"Time works sort of like that, in concertina locomotion."

"Is that a train?"

"No, Roy, it's the way some creatures move, especially tree snakes. They kind of coil and partially uncoil and this motion propels them. I read about it in a nature magazine. You know how a concertina or accordion takes in and lets out air when it's being played? Well, this type of snake looks like that."

"Snakes can see where they're going, can't they?"

"Sure, and they use their tongues as sensors."

"The car's headlights are kind of our sensors."

"I also read that blind people use hand gestures when they talk, the same as people who can see. Isn't that interesting? It has something to do with the way human beings think."

"I think Texas goes on forever."

"We just take it a little bit at a time."

"Like concertina locomotion."

"Yes, baby. As soon as we're east of Houston we'll get a whiff of the bayou. You'll know when we're there with your eyes closed."

Imagine

"**Roy, do you remember** the name of that man in Havana who used to give you a silver dollar whenever he saw you?"

"Sure, Winky. He had two tattoos of a naked girl on his arm."

"Winky Nervo, that's right. It was driving me nuts not being able to remember his name. Winky was in a dream I had last night. What do you mean, he had two tattoos of a naked girl? The same girl?"

"I think so. On one side of the muscle part of his right arm he had the front of the girl and on the underneath was the back of her. She had her hands on her hips the same way in both of the tattoos. I liked Winky a lot. He used to give silver dollars to all the kids."

"For some reason, Winky was in my dream. He was talking to a black woman outside of a restaurant or a bar or a nightclub somewhere, maybe in Havana, though it could have been Mexico City. There was a red and yellow sign flashing on and off behind them. The woman's dress was bright blue, and Winky stood very close to her. Under her, almost. You know how little Winky was, and the woman was very black and much taller. She leaned over hint like a coconut palm."

"I liked Winky, too. Your dad said he was a terrible gambler, threw everything he had away on craps and the horses."

"Why don't we ever see Winky anymore, Mom?"

"Oh, baby, Winky's someplace nobody can find him. He owed a pile of dough to some wrong guys and couldn't pay it back."

"Maybe he's in the old country. Winky always said how when he got set he would go back to the old country and not do anything but eat and drink and forget."

"Honey, Winky's in a country even older than the one he was talk-ing about."

"Maybe he was showing the woman his tattoos. Winky could make the girl's titties jump when he made a muscle."

"Remind me to call your dad tonight when we get to Tampa. You haven't spoken to him for a while."

"Not since my birthday. Mom?"

"Yes, Roy?"

"Winky always had lots of silver dollars in his pockets."

"That doesn't mean he had money, baby. Not real money, anyway."

"Does Dad have real money?"

"He might not have it, but he knows how to find it and where to get it, and that's almost as good. There's a big difference between your father and a man like Winky Nervo. Don't worry about your dad."

"I won't."

"Winky wasn't sharp, Roy. He didn't think ahead."

"It's important, huh? To think ahead."

"Baby, you can't imagine."

Havana, Cuba

The Geography of Heaven

"Do you realize, Roy, that Cairo, Illinois, where we are now, is actually closer to the state of Mississippi than it is to Chicago?"

"I know we're next to the Mississippi River."

"That's right. We were on the Mississippi in St. Louis, Missouri, and now Cairo. From here it flows down to Memphis. What state is Memphis in, baby?"

"Tennessee."

"Good. Then it goes to Greenville—"

"Mississippi."

"Then to New Orleans—"

"Louisiana."

"Before flowing into—"

"The Gulf of Mexico."

"Great, Roy! You really know your geography."

"I think this is the best way to learn it, Mom, by traveling all over. The places are real, then, instead of just dots and names on a map."

"You should show me your maps, Roy, the ones you made up. I'd like to see them."

"I draw maps of real places too, Mom, not just imaginary ones. When we stop, I'll make a map of all the places we've been. Where are we going to stay tonight?"

"I thought we'd see if we could get to A Little Bit O' Heaven, in Kentucky. Remember, they have all those little cottages named after different flowers?"

"Oh, yeah. We stayed in the Rose Cottage because that's Nanny's name."

"There certainly isn't much color in the sky today, is there? It's just grey with tiny specks of black in it."

"It might snow, huh?"

"I think it's more likely to rain, honey. It's not cold enough to snow."

"Mom, if you had a choice between freezing to death or burning up, which one would you choose?"

"I'd take freezing, definitely, because once your body is numb all over, you can't feel anything. You die, sure, but it's better than feeling your flesh melt off the bones. How about you?"

"I like being in hot weather a lot more than cold weather, but I guess you're right. I saw in a movie where a guy who was lost in the wilderness made a blanket of snow for himself and survived until the rescuers came because his body stayed warm under the snow."

"I didn't know about that, Roy. Let's remember it, just in case we get stranded sometime in the mountains in a blizzard."

"You were right, Mom, here comes the rain. All the tiny black spots in the sky were raindrops ready to fall. I never saw rain that looked so black before. It's like being bombed by billions of ants."

"Yes, baby, it is strange, isn't it? Roll up your window all the way. I hope we can make it to A Little Bit O' Heaven before it gets too bad."

"Mom, is there a religion of geography?"

"Not really, unless you consider the ones where people worship places they believe an extraordinary event occurred."

"Probably something important to someone happened just about everywhere, and some people made more of a big deal about it than others."

"Yes, baby, you've got it right."

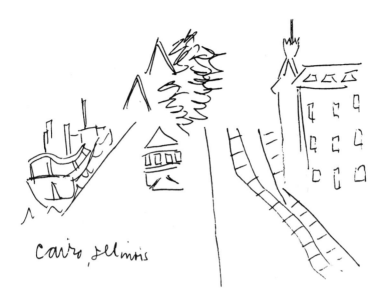

cairo, selimis

Man and Fate

"Vicksburg is really a sad place, Mom, I've never seen so many graves."

"It's spooky here, baby, I agree. It breaks my heart to think about all the young boys, many not too much older than you, who're buried here. You know, Roy, some people would think we're crazy, driving around like this in a cemetery in Mississippi in the rain. I can't help but imagine the lives these boys might have had if there hadn't been a War Between the States. A civil war is the worst kind of war. It's been almost one hundred years since this one ended, and the South still hasn't recovered."

"Soldiers from the North are buried here, too, Mom. Hundreds of 'em."

"How can a place be so dreary and beautiful at the same time?"

"I'll bet there are ghosts here who come out and fight the war all over again every night."

"It wouldn't surprise me, baby. Somebody could make a terrific movie of ghosts or even corpses rising from their graves and not fighting but talking with one another peacefully about how horribly wrong it was to have a war in the first place."

"That wouldn't be so exciting, Mom, not if they were just talking. It would be cool to see the corpses, though."

"The only real reasons people go to war anymore are religion and money, and often it's a combination of the two. In the Civil War, cheap labor in the form of slaves was the main issue. In World War II, Hitler used the Jews as scapegoats for Germany's economic problems, which were a result of World War I. He had to go to war to get Germany out of debt. Do you understand any of this, Roy?"

"Not everything. I know that sometimes people want the land that other people are on."

"That has to do with money. One piece of land might be better than another to grow crops on, or there's oil or gas or diamonds and gold or other valuable minerals in it. And as far as religion is concerned, everybody should be left alone and leave others alone to worship as they please."

"Why don't they?"

"Most do, Roy, but some people get carried away. They believe their way should be the only way. It's when people think they've got an exclusive on being right that the world goes ape."

"I once heard Dad say to a guy, 'If I had to get a job done right and I had to choose between you and an ape to do it, I'd take the ape.'"

"I've had enough of Vicksburg, baby. How about you?"

Where Osceola Lives

"Mom, did you know that the Seminoles are the only Indian tribe that never gave up? They hid out here in the Everglades and the soldiers couldn't defeat them."

"I know that the Glades was much larger then, so the Indians had more room to move around and evade the army."

"The Seminoles weren't really a regular tribe, either. They were made up of renegades and survivors of several different tribes who banded together for a last stand in what they called the Terrible Place. Their leader was Osceola, whose real name was Billy Powell, and he was mostly a white man."

"If I'm not mistaken, Roy, the road to Miami that we're on now was originally a Micosukee Indian trail. Imagine how difficult it must have been to build the highway here."

"Really dangerous, too. There's alligators and panthers and water moccasins all around. The Seminoles somehow survived everything, even swamp fevers that killed dozens of soldiers."

"In the movie *Key Largo*, there are two Seminole brothers who've escaped from jail and the cops are looking for them. Even though he's seen them passing in a canoe, the hotel owner doesn't tell the cops because he likes the brothers and believes they were treated unfairly. Later, just before a hurricane is about to hit, the Seminole brothers and other Indians come to the hotel for shelter, as they'd always done during a big storm, but a gangster who's taken over the hotel refuses to let them in."

"What happens to them?"

"They huddle together on the porch of the hotel and ride it out. The Seminole brothers survive."

"Remember Johnny Sugarland, my favorite alligator wrestler at the reptile farm up in St. Augustine?"

"Sure, baby. The boy with three fingers on one hand and the thumb missing on the other."

"He's a Seminole. Johnny told me about Osceola, so I got a book about him from the school library. Nobody except the Seminoles knows where Osceola's body is buried. Some of them say that Osceola is still alive and hunting with an eagle, an owl, and a one-eyed dog as old as he is way back in a part of the Terrible Place that no white man has ever seen."

"Crazy Horse, the Sioux warrior, is another Indian whose burial place is kept secret. Supposedly, no white man knows where his grave is, either."

"I'd go into the swamp with Johnny, if he'd take me. It would be great to see where Osceola lives."

"I'm sure he's dead now, Roy. For the Seminoles, it's Osceola's spirit that's still alive."

"I think I like the Everglades more than any other place I've been."

"Why is that, baby?"

"It's got the most hiding places of anywhere. If you don't get eaten by a gator or a snake, or get swallowed up in quicksand or die of a fever, you could disappear from everyone for as long as you wanted."

"Roy, there's a reason the Indians called this the Terrible Place."

"I know, Mom, but I think I'd be okay, as long as I remembered the way out."

Suwanee River, Fla.

The Crime of Pass Christian

"You know, Mom, the best time for me is when we're moving in the car. I like it when we're between the places we're coming from and going to."

"Don't you miss your friends, or sleeping in your own bed?"

"Sometimes. But right now we're not in New Orleans yet and it's kind of great that nobody else knows exactly where we are. Where are we, anyway?"

"Comin' up on Pass Christian, honey. Remember once we stayed in a house here for a week when your dad had business in Biloxi? An old two-story house with a big screened-in porch that wrapped all around the second floor."

"It's where I trapped a big brown scorpion under a glass and left it there overnight. In the morning the glass was still upside down but the scorpion was gone. You let it go when I was asleep, didn't you, Mom?"

"No, baby, I told you I didn't. I don't know how it got out. And your dad was away that night in New Orleans. It was a real mystery."

"I like that we don't know what happened. Maybe there's a ghost living in the house who picked up the glass, or somehow the scorpion did it with his poison tail."

"This part of the Gulf Coast always seems haunted to me. If the scorpion had gotten out by itself, the glass would have fallen over, or at least moved. As I recall, it was in exactly the same place the next morning when we looked."

"What kind of ghost do you think lives in that house?"

"Oh, probably the old lady who lived there all of her life. Someone told me she was almost a hundred years old when she died. She never married, and lived alone after her parents passed away."

"What was her name?"

"Baby, I don't remember. Mabel something, I think. There was a story about a kidnapping involving the woman. I can't recall exactly what happened, but she had been kidnapped when she was a child and held for ransom. The family was quite wealthy. It was a famous case."

"Did the police catch the kidnappers?"

"I guess so. Oh, wait, Roy, here's the sharp curve in the highway I hate. I always forget when it's coming up."

"You're a great driver, Mom. I always feel safe in the car with you."

"You shouldn't ever worry when we're driving, baby. Now, look, the road stays pretty straight from here on. Yes, the men who kidnapped Mabel Wildrose—that was the family's name, Wildrose—were caught and sent to prison."

"Did they hurt her?"

"Something bad happened, but it was strange. Mabel Wildrose was nine years old when she was kidnapped."

"The same age as me."

"Yes, your age. They cut off some of little Mabel's hair and sent it to her parents."

"She must have been really scared."

"I'm sure she was. But other than that, I don't think she was harmed. Her parents paid the money and the cops found Mabel wherever it was the kidnappers said she would be."

"You said the men were caught."

"Uh-huh, in New Orleans, when they tried to get on a freighter bound for South America. There was one crazy part of the deal I remember now: The men had left her wrapped in a blanket, and when they were caught trying to board the boat at the dock in New Orleans, one of them was discovered to be carrying Mabel's clothes, including her shoes, in his suitcase. The man had polished the shoes and asked the police if he could keep them with him in his jail cell. He was a nut."

"I wouldn't want to be kidnapped."

"Baby, nobody's going to steal you. Everyone knows who your dad is. They wouldn't want to get into trouble with him."

"What if they didn't want money? What if someone wanted to keep me?"

"It won't happen, Roy, really. Don't worry."

"One day I thought I saw a ghost in the house in Pass Christian, but I don't think it was Mabel Wildrose. It was too big to be her. I was lying on the floor in the front room, playing with my soldiers. It was rainy and kind of dark and cold, and a shadow ran through the room and went out the door. I didn't really see it, it was more like I felt it. The screen door flew open and banged shut behind the shadow."

"Probably only the wind, baby, blowing through the house."

"It might have been the ghost of one of the kidnappers, maybe the guy with Mabel's shoes. Do you think they're dead now?"

"Who, honey?"

"The men who stole Mabel Wildrose when she was nine."

"Oh, they've been dead a long time. They probably died in prison."

"I'd stab someone with my knife if he tried to take me. I'd try to get him in the eye. Probably Mabel didn't have a knife on her, huh, Mom?"

"I doubt that she did, Roy, but sometimes there's not much you can do to stop a person, especially if they're bigger than you."

"I'd wait until they weren't looking and then stab my knife in their eye and run away. They wouldn't catch me if I got outside."

"Forget about it, baby. Nobody is going to kidnap you."

"Sure, Mom, I know. But I'm gonna keep my knife on me anyway."

Cool Breeze

"**What would you do** if one of the men on the chain gang broke away and jumped in our car?"

"That won't happen, Roy. We won't be stopped much longer. Their leg irons are too tough to bust, and these prisoners are swinging bush hooks, not sledgehammers."

"The air is so smoky here. It must be really hard for the men to breathe when it's so hot."

"We're in the Bessemer Cutoff, baby. This part of Alabama is full of steel mills. If these men weren't prisoners, most of them would be working in the mills or mines or blast furnaces somewhere in Jefferson County."

"There are more black guys than white guys on this chain gang. On the last one we passed, in Georgia, there were more white prisoners."

"We're going to move now, honey. Get your head back in."

"Uncle Jack had two brothers working construction for him who'd been on a chain gang. Their names were Royal and Rayal."

"They told you they were in jail?"

"Uh-huh. They didn't murder anybody, only robbed a bank. Tried to, anyway. Rayal, I think it was, told me the reason they got caught was because they didn't have a car. They got the money, then tried to take a bus to get away."

"Where was this?"

"Jacksonville, I think. The bus didn't arrive when it was supposed to, so the cops arrested them."

"I'll never forget that movie with Paul Muni, *I Was a Fugitive from a Chain Gang*. At the end he escapes, and when he meets his old girlfriend, she asks him how he survives. As he disappears into the shadows, he whispers, 'I steal.' It's pretty spooky."

"I feel kind of bad waving back at the chain-gang guys, you know? We get to leave and they don't."

"Here we go. Oh, baby, doesn't it feel good to have a breeze?"

Night Owl

"It's dangerous to drive in the fog like this, isn't it, Mom?"

"We're going slowly, baby, in case we have to stop on a dime."

"Do you know how many bridges there are that connect the islands between Key West and Miami?"

"About forty, I think, maybe more."

"Does everyone have secrets?"

"Oh, yes, certainly they do."

"Do you?"

"One or two."

"Would you die if anybody found them out?"

"I wouldn't die, no. There are just a few things I'd rather other people didn't know."

"Even me?"

"Even you what?"

"You have secrets you wouldn't tell me?"

"Roy, there are things I don't want to think about or remember, things I try to keep secret even from myself."

"It must be hard to keep a secret from yourself."

"Gee, baby, I can't see a thing."

Islamorada

"Listen, baby, tonight when we get to the hotel I want you to call your dad."

"Is he coming to Miami?"

"No, he has to stay in Chicago. Your dad is sick, Roy, he's in the hospital. It'll cheer him up if you call him there."

"What's wrong with him?"

"He's got a problem with his stomach. I think he needs to have an operation."

"I remember when I was in the hospital to have my tonsils out. You stayed in the room with me on a little bed."

"You were such a good patient. After the surgery you opened your mouth to talk but you couldn't. All you could do was whisper."

"The nurse gave me ice cream."

"Poor baby, when the doctor came in you asked him if he would do another operation and put your voice back in."

"Is Dad scared?"

"Your dad doesn't scare easily, honey. He's a pretty tough guy."

"The doctor said I was brave. I didn't cry or anything."

"You were great, Roy. I was the one who was frightened."

"Can we stop at Mozo's in Islamorada and get squid rings?"

"Sure. Oh, there's a big sailboat, Roy. Look! She's a real beauty."

"It's a ketch."

"I never can tell the difference between a ketch and a yawl."

"The mizzenmast is farther forward on a ketch, and the mizzen sail is larger than on a yawl. Uncle Jack taught me."

"You know, I don't think your dad has ever been on a boat in his life, except when he was a little boy and sailed across the Atlantic Ocean with his family from Europe to America."

"How old was he?"

"About eight, I think."

"Did they come on a sailboat?"

"No, baby, on a big ship with lots of people."

"Why did they come?"

"To have a better life. After the big war, the first one, things were very bad where your dad's family lived."

"Were they poor?"

"I guess it was difficult to make a decent living. There were more opportunities over here. The United States was a young country and people from all over, not just Europe but Asia and Africa, too, felt they could build a new life for themselves. Everyone came to America this way, for work and religious reasons. They still do."

"Were you already here when Dad came?"

"I wasn't born yet. Your dad had been here for almost thirty years before we met."

"Dad didn't tell me he was sick."

"He'll pull through, Roy, don't worry. We'll call him as soon as we get to Miami. You'll see, he'll tell you he's going to be all right."

"I wish you and Dad were still married."

"It's better the way things are for your dad and me, baby. Some people just weren't made to live with each other."

"I won't ever get married."

"Don't be ridiculous, Roy. Of course you'll get married. You'll have children and grandchildren and everything. You just have to find the right girl."

"Weren't you the right girl for Dad?"

"He thought I was. It's not so easy to explain, honey. There were all kinds of reasons our marriage didn't work. The best part of it was that we had you."

"If Dad dies, I don't want another one."

"What do you mean, baby?"

"If you get married again, he won't be my dad."

"Look, Roy. Is that one a ketch or a yawl?"

"A yawl. It's got two jibs."

"We'll be in Islamorada in five minutes. I'm ready for some squid rings myself."

On the Arm

"Maybe we can go to a baseball game in Atlanta. I went once with Dad and his friend Buddy from Detroit. We saw the Crackers play the Pelicans."

"We'll look in the newspaper when we get there, baby, and see if the Crackers are in town. Don't hang out of the window, Roy. Get your arms back in."

"Mom, it's so hot. I won't get hit."

"Remember when we read about that boy whose arm got taken off by a truck?"

"Is Buddy from Detroit still in Atlanta?"

"Buddy Delmar, you mean? No, honey, I think he's in Vegas now. He works for Moe Lipsky."

"Buddy was a ballplayer. He knows a lot about baseball."

"Your dad told me Buddy could have had a career in the game, but he had a problem, so he didn't go on."

"What kind of problem?"

"He's a fixer, Roy. I guess he always was, even back when he played. Buddy bet on games. He paid pitchers to let batters get hits, hitters to strike out, and fielders to make errors."

"Did he get caught?"

"Somewhere along the line. I don't know exactly what happened, but according to your dad, Buddy had an umpire on the arm who had a big mouth. The ump spilled the beans and did Buddy in. I don't think he went to jail over it, but he was finished as far as baseball was concerned."

"He could tell me things that would happen before they happened. A player would do something and Buddy'd say, 'Didn't I tell ya?'"

"The first time I met Buddy Delmar, your dad and I were at the

73

Ambassador, in the Pump Room. Buddy paid for our drinks. He flashed a roll that could have choked a horse."

"You mean if he tried to swallow the money."

"Who, honey?"

"The horse."

"It's just an expression, Roy. Buddy likes to act like a big shot. Some women go for that routine, not me."

"I remember Buddy asked me, 'How's that good-looking mother of yours?'"

"Did your dad hear him say that?"

"I think Dad was getting a hot dog."

"Buddy Delmar thinks he's catnip to the ladies."

"I'd never take money to strike out."

"Of course you wouldn't. You won't be like Buddy Delmar. You'll be your own man."

"Is Dad his own man?"

"Sure, Roy, he is. Being his own man causes him problems sometimes."

"Buddy from Detroit had a problem, you said."

"Baby, you don't have to be like any of these people. Your dad is a decent person, don't get me wrong, but he does things you'll never do. Your life will be different, Roy."

"What about Buddy?"

"What about him?"

"Is he a decent person?"

"If Buddy Delmar had never been born, the world wouldn't be any worse off."

"Mom, if we ever have a house, could I get a dog?"

"Oh, Roy, you really are my own special angel. We won't always be living in hotels, I promise. Listen, if the Crackers aren't playing, we'll go to a movie, okay?"

"Okay. It wouldn't have to be a big dog. If he was too big, he wouldn't be happy riding in our car so much."

"Baby, remember what I said about keeping your arms in."

Look Out Below

"Mom, when you were a girl, what did you want to be when you grew up?"

"I thought I might be a singer, like Nanny. Other than that, I had no idea."

"Uncle Jack says I should be an architect, like him."

"If that's what you want to do, baby."

"I want to be a baseball player, but after that I'm not sure."

"Apalachicola. Doesn't the name of this town sound like a train? Let's say it, Roy. Slowly at first, then faster and faster."

"Apalachicola—Apalachicola—Apalachicola Apalachicola—Apalachica-cola—Apalachica-agh!-cola! It gets harder the more times you say it."

"Isn't it just like a choo-choo? Ap-alachi-cola—Ap-alachi-cola—Ap-alachi-cola—"

"It's pretty here, huh, Mom?"

"Especially now, at sundown. Your dad and I were here once in a big storm. Almost a hurricane but not quite. Black sand was flying everywhere. We couldn't see to drive."

"I think it was close to here where Uncle Jack's boat got stuck on a sandbar when he and Skip and I were fishing. Remember, Mom? I told you about it."

"Tell me again, honey. I've forgotten."

"Uncle Jack couldn't drive the boat off the sandbar so he told me and Skip to jump in the water and push from the stern."

"Did it work, or did you have to call the coast guard?"

"It worked, but when we first got in and started pushing, Skip saw

a big fin coming at us. He shouted, 'Shark!' and we climbed back into
the boat as fast as we could. Uncle Jack asked, 'Where's a shark?' Skip
pointed at the place where he'd seen the fin and Uncle Jack said, 'Get
back in the water and push! I'll tell you when there's a shark coming.'"

"That sounds like my brother. Did you both get back in?"

"Uh-huh, Skip's a lot stronger than I am—"

"He's four years older."

"Yeah, well, he pushed as hard as he could and so did I, and Uncle Jack
cut the wheel sharp so the boat came unstuck. Then Skip and I swam
fast to it and climbed aboard before the shark came back."

"I'll have to talk to Jack about this."

"No, Mom, it was okay. We had to do it. We were really stuck and
only Uncle Jack could drive the boat."

"You wouldn't be much good as a baseball player if you lost a leg to
a shark."

"There was a pitcher with the White Sox who only had one leg. I
saw a movie about him. I think he lost it in a war."

"Roy, is this true?"

"Honest, Mom. He pitched on a wooden leg. I don't know how many
times, but he did it."

"That's incredible. A person really can do just about anything if he
works hard at it."

"When I find out what I want to do, I'll work really hard at it."

"After baseball, you mean."

"Yeah, after baseball. Mom?"

"Yes, baby?"

"Do you think Skip and I were really dumb to get back in the water?
What if the shark had come up from underneath to bite us?"

"Please, Roy, even if there was a one-legged baseball player, I don't
want to think about it."

The Up and Up

"Why didn't you tell me Dad was going to die?"

"Oh, baby, I didn't know he would die. I mean, everyone dies sooner or later, but we couldn't know he would die this soon."

"Dad wasn't old."

"No, Roy, he was forty-eight. Too young."

"I didn't know he was in the hospital again."

"We talked to him just after he went back in, don't you remember?"

"I forgot."

"Your dad really loved you, Roy, more than anything."

"He didn't sound sick, that's why I didn't remember he was in the hospital."

"It's a shame he died, baby, really a shame."

"After he came home from the hospital the first time, after his operation, Phil Sharky told me Dad was too tough to die."

"Phil Sharky's not a person worth listening to about anything. I'm sure he meant well telling you that, but he's the kind of man who if you ask him to turn off a light only knows how to break the lamp."

"What does that mean, Mom?"

"I mean Phil Sharky can't be trusted. You can't believe a word he says. If he says it's Tuesday, you can get fat betting it's Friday. Phil Sharky's a crooked cop who doesn't play straight with anyone."

"I thought he was Dad's friend."

"Look how dark the sky's getting, Roy, and it's only two o'clock. If we're lucky, we'll make it to Asheville before the rain hits. I thought we'd stay at the Dixieland Hotel. It has the prettiest views of the Smokies."

"Phil Sharky gave me his gun to hold once. It was really heavy. He said to be careful because it was loaded."

"Was your dad there?"

"No, he went out with Dummy Fish and left me at the store. He told me he'd be right back. I asked Phil if the gun wouldn't weigh so much if there weren't any bullets in it and he said if they went where they were supposed to it wouldn't."

"Baby, you won't ever see Phil Sharky again if I have anything to do with it. Did you tell your dad about this? That Phil let you handle his gun?"

"Dad didn't get back for a long time and I fell asleep on the newspaper bundles. When I woke up, Phil was gone and Dad and Dummy and I went to Charmette's for pancakes. I remember because Solly Banks was there and he came over to our table and said I was a lucky kid to have the kind of father who'd take me out for pancakes at four in the morning."

"Suitcase Solly, another character who couldn't tell the up and up if it bit him. So your dad didn't know Sharky showed you the gun?"

"Phil told me not to say anything to Dad, in case he wouldn't like the idea, so I didn't."

"We're not gonna beat the rain, baby, but we'll get there while there's still light. Tomorrow we'll fly to Chicago. The funeral's on Sunday."

"Will everyone be there?"

"I don't know about everyone, but your dad knew a lot of people. Most of the ones who come will want to talk to you."

"Even people I don't know?"

"Probably. All you have to do is thank them for paying their respects to your father."

"What if I cry?"

"It's normal to cry at a funeral, Roy. Don't worry about it."

"Mom, what was the last thing Dad said before he died?"

"Gee, baby, I really don't know. I think when the nurse came to give him a shot for the pain, he'd already died in his sleep. There was nobody in the room."

"Do you remember the last thing he said to you?"

"Oh, I think it was just to not worry, that he'd be okay."

"I bet Dad knew he was dying and he didn't want to tell us."

"Maybe so."

"What if he got scared just before he died? Nobody was there for him to talk to."

"Don't think about it, Roy. Your dad didn't live very long, but he enjoyed himself."

"Dad was on the up and up, wasn't he, Mom?"

"Your dad did things his own way, but the important thing to remember, baby, is that he knew the difference."

Black Space

"Isn't that terrible? Roy, did you hear that just now on the radio?"

"I wasn't really listening Mom. I'm reading the story of Ferdinand Magellan. Did you know there's a cloud named after him that's a black space in the Milky Way? What happened?"

"They found two cut-up bodies in suitcases in the left-luggage department in the railway station in New Orleans."

"Do they know who put them there?"

"The attendant told police it was a heavyset, middle-aged white woman who wore glasses and a black raincoat with what looked like orange paint stains on it."

"It's raining now. When it rains in Louisiana, everything gets fuzzy."

"What do you mean, things get fuzzy?"

"The drops are wobbly on the windows and that makes shapes outside weird."

"People are capable of anything, baby, you know that? The problem is you can never really know who you're dealing with, like this woman who chopped up those bodies."

"Were they children?"

"Who? The corpses in the suitcases?"

"Uh-huh."

"No, honey, I'm sure they were adults."

"But the crazy lady who did it is loose."

"They'll get her, Roy, don't worry. Maybe not right away, but they will."

"Do you think it's easy to kill someone, Mom?"

"What a strange question to ask. I don't know. I suppose for some people it is."

"Could you do it?"

"Maybe with a gun if I were being threatened. I've never really thought about it."

"Could you cut up a body like she did?"

"Roy, stop it. Of course not. Let's talk about something else. Are you hungry? We can stop in Manchac and get fried catfish at Middendorf's."

"I wonder if she wrapped the body parts up so blood didn't go everywhere."

"Please, baby. I'm sorry I mentioned it."

"Remember the shrunken head Uncle Jack brought back from New Guinea?"

"How could I forget?"

"Somebody had to chop it off before it got shrunk. Or do you think the whole body was shrunk first?"

"Roy, that's enough."

"I bet that attendant was really surprised when he saw what was inside those suitcases."

"They must have begun to smell badly so the attendant got suspicious. I think he called the police, though, and they opened the suitcases."

"Do you think the woman is still in New Orleans?"

"Baby, how would I know? Maybe she just took a train and beat it out of town. I'm sure she did. She's probably in Phoenix, Arizona, by now."

"Nobody really has control over anybody else, do they?"

"A lot of people don't have control over themselves, that's how a horrible thing like this can happen. Now stop thinking about it. Think about horses, Roy, how beautiful they are when they run."

"Mom, you won't leave me alone tonight, okay?"

"No, baby, I won't go out tonight. I promise."

Ball Lightning

It was late afternoon of a late-spring day. The rural two-lane next to which stood a two-pump filling station was empty. The faint sound of an approaching car could be heard, a dim buzz that became louder and louder until a sparkling new blue Ford Sunliner convertible with the top down pulled up at the pumps. A young blond woman sat behind the steering wheel. She pressed the horn several times, until an attendant emerged from the station garage. The attendant, dressed in grimy gray overalls and a red baseball cap, stepped around to the driver's side of the Ford.

"You must be in a hurry."

"Fill it up."

"Regular or ethyl?"

"Ethyl, I guess."

"Pretty automobile."

"I guess."

"Machine inside has soft drinks. Mostly Nehi. Grape, orange, and root beer."

"Just fill it, okay?"

The attendant walked over to the ethyl pump, rotated the handle to activate it, took down the hose, unscrewed the Ford's gas cap, inserted the hose nozzle, and began fueling the car.

"Hey," said the driver, "how far am I from Superior?"

"The lake?"

"No, the town."

"Forty, forty-five miles. But you won't get there this way."

"I thought this was the road to Superior."

"Twenty-one."

"This is State Route 15, isn't it?"

"Uh-huh."

"So what's twenty-one?"

"Your age. I'm guessing."

"I'll be twenty-two next month. Look, you mean this isn't the way to Superior?"

"Not anymore. Used to be, though."

The driver got out of the car. She was wearing a thin, sleeveless dress. A wind picked up, blowing her yellow hair around her face. She walked to the rear of the car and looked at the attendant.

"Hey, you're a girl."

"So?"

"Nothin'. Just I've never seen a girl gas jockey before."

"Now you have."

"You alone here?"

"Yeah, My Uncle Ike owns this station. He's sick today."

"The president?"

"Yeah, of the Black Fork Elks."

"Bad heart?"

"Uh-huh. How'd you know?"

"How old are you?"

"Eighteen. Nineteen next month."

"What day?"

"The fourteenth. You?"

"Me?"

"Your birthday. It's next month, too, you said."

"The fourteenth."

"That's pretty cool, I think. Our birthday is the same!"

"I'm older, though."

"Only three years."

The attendant removed the hose nozzle from the car and replaced it on the pump. She reattached the gas cap, then moved closer to the driver and extended her right hand.

"My name is Amelia."

The driver hesitated, then shook Amelia's hand.

"Terry."

Amelia took off her cap, allowing her abundant black hair to drop to her shoulders.

"You have gorgeous hair."

"Thanks. I ought to cut it. Gets in the way when I'm workin' on engines. Do you want to come inside and have a drink? Or maybe I'll bring some out. What flavor would you like? My favorite's grape."

"Orange, please."

Amelia went inside and Terry wandered over to the front of the station office and sat down in one of two adjacent flamingo chairs. Amelia came out, handed Terry a bottle of orange soda pop, and sat down in the other chair, holding her bottle of grape pop.

"What's in Superior?"

"My boyfriend."

"That his car?"

"Yes. He left it with me up in Pigeon River."

"That where you're from?"

"My parents have a house there. I live in Chicago."

"I've never been in Chicago. I was in Pigeon River once, though. As a child. Don't hardly remember much, except for the falls. My brother, Priam, and I walked across the falls on a skinny, shaky little wooden bridge. Both ways. I was seven."

"Your brother's name is Priam?"

"Uh-huh. His nickname was Tick."

"Was?"

"Maybe it still is, I don't know. He disappeared on us six years ago, when he turned twenty-one."

"Disappeared? You mean you don't know where he is?"

Amelia took a long swig from her bottle.

"Haven't seen or heard from him since. Bet he doesn't know our folks died, either."

"I'm sorry. How did they die? If you don't mind my asking."

"Plane crash. They were flying down from Huron to Black Fork in Daddy's boss's Cessna. Mr. Herbert. He was flyin'—Mr. Herbert, that is—and there was a violent thunderstorm. A big red ball of lightning struck the plane. That's what a farmer said who saw it happen. Said there was a loud bang, like a rifle shot, as a fireball collided with the Cessna. Broke the damn plane apart, my mother and father and Mr. Herbert, too. They all of 'em rained down from the sky in pieces."

"My boyfriend?"

"What about him?"

"His name is Priam. His real name. Everyone calls him Pete. Pete Farnsworth."

Amelia dropped her bottle onto the ground. The soda pop spilled out.

"That's my name. Farnsworth. There can't be another Priam. It was our mother's grandfather's name. How old is he?"

"Twenty-seven."

"Does his left eye wander?"

Terry nodded.

"I don't believe this," she said.

"He in Superior?"

"Yes. We're going to drive together to Chicago. Pete had some business there, Superior."

"What does he do?"

"He sells paper products."

Amelia was crying. Terry leaned over to comfort her, putting her bottle on the ground.

"Tick and Uncle Ike were really close when Tick was a boy. He was closer with Uncle Ike than with our dad."

"We can call him, Amelia. Priam, I mean. Do you have a telephone here?"

"What for? I guess he didn't want anything more to do with us."

Amelia stopped crying.

"Look," she said, "don't tell him you met me, okay?"

"But your parents—he'll want to know what happened to them."

"No, probably not. Not about any of us. I'll tell Uncle Ike, that's all."

"Why would Pete—Priam—Tick—run off like that?"

"What's he told you about his family?"

"That he was an only child. That his parents are both dead."

"He won't be lying now."

"Amelia, come with me to Superior. I'm sure your brother will want to see you."

Amelia stood up.

"You must've been a lot of places," she said. "I mean, travelin' around."

"Not so much before I met your brother. He travels quite a bit for business, and I go along sometimes. How did he get that nickname, Tick?"

"I always knew him as that. It was from before I was born. Uncle Ike played a game with him when he was little, to teach Tick how to tell time. I don't know exactly how it worked, but Uncle Ike would point at a clock and look at my brother and Priam would say, 'Tick!' Then Uncle Ike would say, 'Tock!' And Priam would say, 'Six o'clock!' Or whatever time it was. Anyway, after that everyone just called him Tick."

"It's strange how you think you know someone, know him completely, and then discover you don't. I know people compartmentalize their lives, they keep secrets, everyone does. But this scares me a little."

"You feel betrayed, huh?"

"I don't know if betrayed is exactly the right word. I'm not sure I have the right to feel betrayed. Maybe he's got a good reason for burying all this. What about you?"

"Me?"

"Yes. Don't you feel betrayed? After all, your brother did abandon you, didn't he?"

"I suppose he did. For a while, anyway."

"Here he's been in Chicago all this time and never contacted you. Closer, even, in Superior. He's driven right past this place without stopping."

"You make him sound so . . . so . . . vile. Tick was always sweet to me. He was a good brother."

"Past tense."

"The summer my friend Lolly and I were thirteen, we went swimmin' one day at Foster's Pond and it started rainin', thunderin' and lightnin'. We took off runnin' for home. A car stopped on the road and the driver offered us a lift. It was a man we didn't know, he was about fifty. Ordinarily we never would have taken it, but being that it was pourin' down buckets and the sky was crashin' and all electric and everything, we got in. Besides, he was an old guy. I figured he couldn't be too dangerous."

Terry clucked her tongue.

"Lolly got in the front seat with him and I got in the back. He didn't say much, as I recall. We were ridin' along and all of a sudden Lolly let out with the loudest scream I have ever heard. She jumped over into the backseat with me, and yelled, 'Stop this car! Stop it right now!' The old guy hit the brakes and skidded to a stop right in the road and Lolly grabbed my hand and pulled me out the rear/door on her side. We ran off into the woods and hid until we were sure the car was gone."

"Did he touch her?"

"No. Lolly said she looked over and there was his big old hairy thing hangin' out of his pants."

"It could've been worse. What's it got to do with your brother?"

"What you were sayin', I think. Feelin' of bein' betrayed, or almost. Lolly and me trusted that man to give us a ride out of the storm and he made it into another thing altogether."

"Thing a girl doesn't need to think about. Girls your and Lolly's age."

"That'll be six dollars and twenty cents for the gas."

Terry stood up.

"Amelia, please."

"After a lightning ball explodes, it leaves a kind of mist in the air. The farmer who saw Mr. Herbert's plane go down said that afterwards there was a red fog all around where it happened. It wasn't rainin' except for the body parts and pieces of metal."

"Could I—"

"Six-twenty."

Terry walked to he car and took some money out of her purse, which she had left on the front seat. She brought it to Amelia.

Amelia looked at the bills and took them.

"I'll get your change."

She went into the station office. Terry waited outside. Amelia came back out and handed Terry several coins.

"Thanks for stopping."

"Look, Amelia, what can I do?"

"If you want to get to Superior, go back in the direction you came from on 15 until you hit State Road 8. That's about a mile west of Victory. Go south on 8 to Highway 12 East. Take 12 all the way to the fork. Left is Badgertown, right is Superior. If you get going, you might make it before dark."

Terry started to say something, then put the change into her purse and walked to the car. She got in, started it up, and pulled around the pumps. Amelia walked over to the flamingo chairs and sat down in the one she had been sitting in before. She watched Terry drive away.

A telephone rang inside the station. Amelia got up, went inside, and answered it.

"Ike's Service. Hi, Uncle Ike. How're you feeling? Did you take your pills? No, not much. A few fill-ups, that's all. I've been workin' on Oscar Wright's tranny, mostly. The Olds Holiday, right, A strange thing did happen, though. Woman in a snazzy new Sunliner stopped. No, no, just a fill-up. But she had a story about Tick. Uh-huh. Twenty-two next month, the same day as mine. Yes, how do you like that? I know, sure. Said he's livin' in Chicago, workin' as a paper salesman. Me neither. Right. My thoughts exactly. I never have believed it. Daddy wasn't that way or he would have done it to me is what I think. No way we ever can. Sure. You take good care now, Uncle Ike. I'll see you in two hours, could be less. I'm gonna take another crack at that tranny. Just rest, it's good. I'll fix supper. 'Bye now."

Amelia hung up the telephone. She walked outside and stood next to the flamingo chairs. She put her left foot on the back of the one Terry had been sitting in and kicked it over.

Written by Roy's mother in the Black Hawk Motel, Oregon, Illinois, 1958.

Chief Blackhawk

Fear and Desire

"I don't like when the sky gets dark so early."

"That's what happens in the winter, Roy. The days are a lot shorter and colder because our side of the planet is farther away from the sun."

"The trees look beautiful without leaves, don't they, Mom?"

"I like when it's sunny and cold. It makes my skin feel so good. We'll stop soon, baby, in Door County. I'm a little tired."

"I think I dream better in winter."

"Maybe because you sleep more."

"Mom, what do you think of dreams?"

"What do I think of them?"

"Yeah. I mean, what are they? Are they real?"

"Sure, they're real. Sometimes you find out things in dreams that you can't any other way."

"Like what?"

"Some experts think dreams are wishes. You dream about what you really want to happen."

"Once I dreamed that I was running in a forest and wolves were chasing me. There was a real big red wolf that caught me in deep snow and started eating one of my legs. Then I woke up. I didn't want that to happen."

"Maybe it meant something else. Also, dreams depend on what's happening around you at the time. Dreams are full of symbols."

"What's a symbol?"

"Something that represents something else, like the red wolf in your dream. The red wolf was a symbol of a fear or desire."

"I was afraid of the wolf because I didn't want him to bite me."

"Do you remember anything else about the dream?"

"The red wolf didn't have any eyes, only dark holes where his eyes were supposed to be."

"This sounds like a case for Sigmund Freud."

"Is he a detective?"

"No, baby, he was a doctor who studied dreams and wrote about them."

"If I'd had a gun I would have shot that wolf."

"It's not always so easy to get rid of something that's chasing you, because it's inside your own mind."

"You mean the red wolf is hiding in my brain?"

"Don't worry, Roy, the wolf won't bother you again. You woke up before he could hurt you."

"The sky's all dark now. Mom, is desire bad or good?"

"It can be either, depending on what it is and why a person desires something."

"A person can't decide not to dream."

"No, baby, dreams either come or they don't. We'll stay at the Ojibway Inn. Remember that motel with the Indian thief on the sign?"

"I bet everybody has scary dreams sometimes."

"Of course they do."

"I hope the red wolf is chasing somebody else now."

God's Tornado

"Oh, Roy, I just love this song. I'll turn it up."

"What is it?"

"'Java Jive' by the Ink Spots. Listen: 'I love java sweet and hot, whoops Mr. Moto, I'm a coffee pot.'"

"That's crazy, Mom. What's it mean?"

"'I love the java and the java loves me.' It's just a silly little song that was popular when I was a girl. Coffee's called java because coffee beans come from there."

"Where?"

"The island of Java, near Borneo."

"Borneo's where the wild men are."

"It's part of Indonesia. Coffee wakes you up, makes you feel jivey, you know, jumpy."

"Who's Mr. Moto?"

"Peter Lorre played him in the movies. He was a Japanese detective."

"Why is he in the song?"

"I don't have the faintest, baby. I guess just because he was a popular character at the time, before the war."

"Look, Mom, there's tree branches all over the road."

"Sit back, honey, I don't want you to bump your head."

"There must have been a big windstorm."

"This part of the country is called Tornado Alley. I don't know why people would live here, especially in trailers. It's always the trailers that get destroyed by tornadoes."

"Where were we when a tornado made all those rocks fall on our car?"

"Kansas. Wasn't that terrible? There were hundreds of dents on the roof and the hood, and we had to get a new windshield."

"Where does weather come from?"

"From everywhere, baby. The wind starts blowing in the middle of the Arabian Sea or the South China Sea or somewhere, and stirs up the waves. Pretty soon there's a storm and clouds form and the planet rotates and spins so the rain or snow works its way around and melts or hardens depending on the temperature."

"Does the temperature depend on how close you are to heaven or hell?"

"No, Roy, heaven and hell have nothing to do with the weather. What matters most is where a place is in relation to the equator."

"I know where that is. It's a line around the globe."

"The nearer to the equator, the hotter it is."

"I think hell must be on the equator, Mom. The ground opens up like a big grave and when the planet turns all the bad people fall in."

"How do good people get to heaven?"

"A whirly wind called God's Tornado comes and picks them up and takes them there. People disappear all the time after a tornado."

"And what about purgatory, the place where people are that God hasn't decided about yet?"

"I think they wait on the planet until God or the Devil chooses them."

"Are they kept in any particular place?"

"I'm not sure. Maybe they just stay where they are, and they don't even know they're waiting."

"I don't know if you know it, baby, but what you say makes perfect sense. I wish I could write down some of these things, or we had a tape recorder to keep them."

"Don't worry, Mom, I've got a good memory. I won't forget anything."

Rome–Paris–San Francisco
April–November 1998

Books by Barry Gifford

FICTION

Do the Blind Dream?
American Falls: The Collected Short Stories
Wyoming
My Last Martini
The Sinaloa Story
Baby Cat-Face
Arise and Walk
Night People
Port Tropique
Landscape with Traveler
A Boy's Novel
The Sailor & Lula Novels:
    Wild at Heart
    Perdita Durango
    Sailor's Holiday
    Sultans of Africa
    Consuelo's Kiss
    Bad Day for the Leopard Man

NONFICTION

Out of the Past: Adventures in Film Noir
Las Cuatro Reinas (with David Perry)
Bordertown (with David Perry)
The Phantom Father: A Memoir
A Day at the Races: The Education of a Racetracker
Saroyan: A Biography (with Lawrence Lee)
The Neighborhood of Baseball
Jack's Book: An Oral Biography of Jack Kerouac (with Lawrence Lee)
Brando Rides Alone

POETRY

Back in America
Replies to Wang Wei
Ghosts No Horse Can Carry
Giotto's Circle
Flaubert at Key West
Beautiful Phantoms
Horse hauling timber out of Hokkaido forest
Poems from Snail Hut
Persimmon: Poems for Paintings
Selected Poems of Francis Jammes (translations with Bettina Dickie)
The Boy You Have Always Loved
Coyote Tantras
The Blood of the Parade

PLAYS

Hotel Room Trilogy

SCREENPLAY

Lost Highway (with David Lynch)

ANTHOLOGY

The Rooster Trapped in the Reptile Room: A Barry Gifford Reader

About the Author

Barry Gifford's novels have been translated into twenty-five languages. His book *Night People* was awarded the Premio Brancati in Italy, and he has been the recipient of awards from PEN, the National Endowment for the Arts, the American Library Association, and the Writers Guild of America. David Lynch's film *Wild at Heart*, which was based on Gifford's novel, won the Palme d'Or at the Cannes Film Festival in 1990; Gifford's novel *Perdita Durango* was made into a feature film by Spanish director Alex de la Iglesia in 1997. Gifford cowrote with director David Lynch the film *Lost Highway* (1997) and cowrote with director Matt Dillon the film *City of Ghosts* (2003). Gifford's recent books include *The Phantom Father*, named a *New York Times* Notable Book of the Year; *Wyoming*, named a *Los Angeles Times* Novel of the Year; *American Falls: The Collected Short Stories*; and *The Rooster Trapped in the Reptile Room: A Barry Gifford Reader*. His writings have appeared in *Punch, Esquire, Rolling Stone, Sport*, the *New York Times, El País, Reforma, La Repubblica, Projections*, and many other publications. He lives in the San Francisco Bay Area. Visit www.barrygifford.com for more information.